Dil in a Pickle

Based on the TV series *Rugrats®* created by Arlene Klasky, Gabor Csupo, and Paul Germain as seen on Nickelodeon®

ISBN 0-439-26236-4

12 11 10 9 8 7 6 5 4 3 2 1   0 1 2 3 4 5/0

Printed in the U.S.A.

First Scholastic printing, January 2001

The babies tiptoed quietly to the big green door. Chuckie was last in line. As they got closer to the room, the green door started to open slowly. The babies all froze. Out of the room came three funny-looking people. They were all dressed in green costumes with pointy ears and big eyes. They looked like . . . aliens!

Rugrats Chapter Books

by Kim Ostrow and Maria Rosado
illustrated by Gary Fields

SCHOLASTIC INC.

New York Toronto London Auckland Sydney
Mexico City New Delhi Hong Kong

Chapter 1

Stu and Didi Pickles were finishing the last bite of their lunch. As they chewed happily, Grandpa Lou rushed into the kitchen. "I hope you two are sitting down," he said. "Because you are not going to believe what I have here in my hands!"

Grandpa Lou was as excited as Stu and Didi had ever seen him. He was waving a small white envelope over his head.

"What is it, Pop?" Stu asked, wiping some bread crumbs off his chin.

"Yes, tell us! What's so exciting?" Didi asked, getting excited herself.

Spike the dog opened a sleepy eye.

"It all started many, many years ago, when I was a little sprout," Grandpa Lou began.

Stu and Didi leaned in and listened carefully. Spike went back to sleep.

"Every lunch my mother ever made me came with a nice, juicy green pickle. But not just any pickle. It was a Rocket Pickle," Grandpa said dreamily. "Why, I can taste them just by saying the name."

"Wow," said Stu. "They sound delicious!"

"Did they stop making them?" Didi asked.

"I believe they did," said Grandpa. "Until just a few weeks ago! You see, I saw that the makers of Rocket Pickles were holding a contest. They were looking for a little sprout to put on every pickle jar and poster they make. The winner of the contest gets a lifetime supply of delicious Rocket Pickles! So I took my favorite snapshot of little Dil and I sent it in!" Grandpa said excitedly. "When they saw his baby face, they knew he was a natural! Our little Dil Pickles is going to be a huge star!"

"Our little Dil won the contest, huh?" Stu said, smiling from ear to ear.

"Yessirree! Photo shoot is today!"

"Today!" said Didi. "Stu and I are signed up for the annual Our Babies, Ourselves Workshop at the Lipschitz Institute. We're very excited about it. I'm afraid we can't take Dil!"

Grandpa thought for a moment. "I'll be happy to take all the sprouts myself. It's not every day a Pickles becomes a star," Grandpa said.

"Well," said Didi, "this contest is just wonderful. But you know, contest or not, I think both our children are stars."

Stu put his arm around Didi. They smiled at each other.

"True as that may be," said Grandpa, "our Dil Pickles is going to be a huge star today. As the advertisement says, 'Rocket Pickles Are Outta This World!'"

Chapter 2

"Did you hear that, Tommy?" said Chuckie Finster, clutching his Reptar doll. "Your grandpa said that your little brother is gonna be a huge star today!"

The babies were playing in the room next to the kitchen.

"Wow," said Tommy. "My little brother is going to be a star!"

"He's going to be very sparkly," said Lil.

"He's going to be shiny, Lillian," said Phil.

"Sparkly, Philip!"

"Shiny!"

"Sparkly!"

"My brother is gonna be the bestest star there is," Tommy said proudly.

"I don't know what you dumb babies are all excited about," said a voice from the doorway.

It was Angelica. She had been standing outside the kitchen and had heard all about the contest too. "You babies don't understand nothing!" she told them.

"Whaddya mean, Angelica?" asked Tommy.

"Do I gotta explain everything around here?" she snapped. "If Dil becomes a star, where do you think he's gonna live?"

The babies thought about it.

"He'll live with all the other prettyful stars," said Lil.

"And where do you think that is?" asked Angelica.

"In the sky?" Chuckie asked nervously.

Angelica smiled slyly. "In outside space!" she said loudly. "The pickle people are going to send Dil and his stinky diapie all the way to outside space. And that's where he'll live forever and ever and ever."

Phil and Lil gasped. Chuckie hid behind his Reptar doll.

"I don't believe you, Angelica," said Tommy. "How do you know he's going to live in outside space forever and ever?"

"Listen," she said. "I got Astronaut Cynthia for Christmas and I know lots about outside space. I'm gonna let you babies in on a little secret."

The babies gathered around Angelica.

"The way a person becomes a star is very simple," said Angelica. "They gotta go to this big room. Then they get makeup and stuff on them to make them look shiny. Then they gots a big camera that they point on you, and when it's time, a person yells, 'Shoot!' A bright light flashes and turns you into a star and shoots you into outside space."

"Oh, Tommy," said Chuckie. "That sounds bad!"

Tommy knew he had to do something. There was no way he was going to let his little brother be thrown into outer space for the rest of his life.

"A baby's gotta do what a baby's gotta do," said Tommy. "And I gotta save my baby brother!"

"We'll help!" said Phil and Lil.

"Gee, Tommy," muttered Chuckie. "I dunno. It sounds kinda scary."

"We can do it, Chuckie!" Tommy told him. "We're going to stop Dil from becoming a star, no matter what!"

Chapter 3

Grandpa Lou was as excited as a sprout in a pickle factory as he looked around the lobby of the photo studio. He couldn't believe his grandson was going to be a star! A man with a big mustache handed him a bunch of forms to fill out.

As Grandpa Lou started on the paperwork, Dil was sleeping soundly in his stroller. The babies were quiet. They had a lot on their minds.

Angelica didn't like waiting. When Grandpa Lou wasn't looking, she stomped over to a big yellow door and poked her head in. Inside she saw a huge room that was decorated to look like outer space. Lots of people were running around and yelling and setting things up. And there, right in the middle of the room, surrounded by cameras and lights, was a big rocket ship shaped like a pickle!

Just then Angelica got an idea. I'm better looking than any stinky baby, she thought to herself. I should be the star!

The more Angelica thought about it, the more she couldn't understand why any company would want a dumb baby on their pickle jars when they could have a beautiful princess like her instead.

"What's in there, Angelica?" asked

Tommy, coming up behind her. "Is it outside space?"

"Do I gotta explain everything around here?" she snapped. Angelica peeked back into the room. She needed a plan to get Dil out of the picture. After all, he may have won the contest, Angelica thought, but I am going to be the star!

"Do ya think there are aliums in there, Tommy?" Chuckie asked nervously, joining his best friend next to the yellow door.

"I don't know, Chuckie. But if there are, I'm sure Angelica will scare them away!" Tommy said.

"Maybe there's outside space dirt in there to eat," said Phil.

"Or space worms!" shouted Lil happily.

Angelica shut the door quietly and put her hands on her hips. "Just as I thought," she muttered.

"What's in there, Angelica?" asked Chuckie. "Aliums?"

Angelica rolled her eyes. Then she bent down to whisper. The babies all gathered close to her. "I'm only gonna say this once, babies, so listen up. Behind that door is a waiting room for outside space."

"A what?" asked Phil.

"Everything that's in that room is waiting its turn to get shot into outside space. It's like when you wait in the room before you go to see the doctor."

Chuckie started to get more nervous. He didn't like the doctor. He especially didn't like getting shots!

"If it's only for people who are going to outside space," said Tommy, "how are we going to get in there to save Dil?"

Angelica rubbed her chin and thought for a moment. "They also let

dumb babies in to say good-bye to their brothers," she answered.

Angelica couldn't wait one more moment to get inside that photo studio. She was sure that when the photographer saw her, he would change his mind instantly and want her to be the star. He would drop Dil like a hot pickle! Once she was in the room, no one would even remember Dil.

"Where are you going, Angelica?" asked Lil.

"I'm gonna go in first. They let older kids in whenever they want. We don't cry and make as much noise as you babies."

And with that, Angelica shut the door behind her.

Tommy was starting to feel a little nervous. But when he looked at his little brother, he knew what he had to do. He would not let him get shot into space, no matter what happened.

All of a sudden, the door opened.

"Dil Pickles!" shouted a loud voice. "We're ready for the Dil Pickles shoot!"

The babies gasped. They had to save Dil—and fast!

Chapter 4

Grandpa Lou and the babies filed into the photo studio. There were bright lights everywhere.

"Tommy, are those the lights that they use to shoot Dil into outside space?" asked Chuckie.

"I hope not!" replied Tommy.

While the babies were looking around the huge room, a man came up to Grandpa Lou and Dil. "Right this way to the greenroom, Mr. Pickles," the man said, escorting them through a big green door.

"Whaddya think that room is for?" Chuckie asked as they watched the door close behind Dil.

"I'll tell you what that room is for, Finster," whispered Angelica. "That's the room where they turn people into aliums!"

"Aliums?! I wanna go home!" cried Chuckie.

"We gots to get Dil before we can go home," Tommy told him. "Don't worry, Chuckie. It won't be scary. Maybe it'll be fun!"

Meanwhile, Angelica had spotted a makeup table that was spilling over with tubes of lipstick and containers of bright powder. If she was going to get the photographer's attention, it wouldn't hurt to be even more beautiful than usual, she thought.

"Makeup is a girl's best friend," Angelica said as she rubbed bright red lipstick all over her lips. "And lips stick is very important for photo shoots."

"I look beeeyooteeful," Angelica said to herself as she patted her nose with a giant pink powder puff. She was sure she'd be a star in no time at all.

On the other side of the studio, the babies were huddled together near the door of the greenroom.

"But, Tommy, if we go in there and get Dil, we'll be turned into aliums!" said Chuckie. "Then we'll never get to see our mommies and daddies again! Or Reptar, either!"

"Whaddya think aliums eat?" asked Phil.

"Worms!" shouted Lil.

"Worms!" shouted Lil.

"All I know is, if my brother gets shot into outside space, I'll never get to see *him* again," said Tommy. "Are ya with me, guys?"

The babies nodded.

All of a sudden Angelica stormed over to the babies. "You babies better keep it down!" she whispered. "Photographers like it to be quiet on the set!"

"We're gonna go rescue Dil," Tommy said proudly.

"Well, don't mess it up," said Angelica. With her new plan, she needed the babies' help. If they took away Dil, the photographer would definitely need a new star. And Angelica would be ready! "I'd hate to see you lose your little brother. The house would be awfully quiet with only one noisy baby around," she added for good measure.

The babies tiptoed quietly to the big green door. Chuckie was last in line. As they got closer to the room, the green door started to open slowly. The babies all froze. Out of the room came three funny-looking people. They were all dressed in green costumes with pointy ears and big eyes. They looked like . . . aliens!

"This shoot is taking forever!" said one of the aliens.

"I can't wait to go already!" said another.

"I tell you, the greenroom sure feels crowded with that baby," said the third one. "Babies should have their own space."

The babies gulped. Those aliens were talking about Dil!

"Didja hear that, Tommy? There's an outside space just for babies!" whispered

Chuckie. "Maybe we should get out of here!"

Tommy looked around nervously. He knew he didn't have much time left to save his brother. He noticed Angelica by the makeup table.

Suddenly Tommy had an idea! He knew they had to get into the greenroom. Maybe if the babies already *looked* liked aliens, no one would turn them *into* aliens!

"All we gotta do, guys," Tommy said, "is put some of that green makeup on us. Then no one will be able to tell that we are babies!"

The babies were excited by Tommy's plan. Even Chuckie thought that putting green makeup on his face might be fun. He might look like Reptar!

At the makeup table, the babies set to work. Lil decorated Phil with green eye shadow. Tommy painted Chuckie with something sparkly. Powdered makeup made huge, dusty clouds over their heads.

"Yum! This lipsticle tastes better than crayons!" cried Phil.

"You look prettyful, Chuckie," said Lil. "Just like Reptar."

"Gee, thanks, Lil," Chuckie said, grinning shyly.

"We're almost done, guys," said Tommy. "Dil will be home safe and sound in no time!"

The babies put the finishing touches on each other. When they decided they looked perfect, they started again toward the greenroom.

"Follow me, guys," said Tommy. "And remember, if anyone asks, we're aliums!"

Chapter 5

Meanwhile, Angelica was standing in the middle of the studio, smiling at the photographer. "Ahem," she said.

But the photographer didn't hear her.

"Excuse me," she said sweetly.

But the photographer walked right by her.

This was going to be harder than she'd thought! Knowing that she had a beautiful singing voice, Angelica tried bursting into song. "Tinkle, Tinkle, Little star, I know how and where you are . . ."

Obviously the photographer didn't know talent when he saw it, because he walked away. Angelica stomped her foot. No one was going to stop her chance at stardom just like that. She just had to try a little harder.

She tried singing. She tried tap dancing. She even did a cartwheel. But no matter how hard she tried, the photographer just wouldn't notice her.

Then, while doing an extra-special bunny hop, Angelica knocked over a big shiny light.

Finally he looked at her! Now was her big chance.

Angelica flashed him her best smile. "My name's Angelica," she said.

The photographer frowned. "Why don't you have a seat, young lady," he said, pointing to his personal chair.

Angelica beamed. She was happier than the day she got her Astronaut Cynthia doll. The photographer had not only noticed her beauty, he wanted her to sit close by! Angelica was as close to being a star as she'd ever dreamed. It would only be a matter of minutes before she was asked to be the model for Rocket Pickles.

Angelica sat still for as long as she could. But stardom was calling, and Angelica wanted to get there faster. "Mr. Photographer," she said.

He looked down at her.

"Well, sir," she started. "My name is Angelica Pickles, and I'm going to be a model. Ever since I got my first Fashion Model Cynthia, I knew I would be perfect at it. I also am very smart. And I like pickles—a lot!" She smiled and batted her eyelashes.

"You are something else," he said.

"I know," said Angelica. She was happy he was finally seeing things her way. "So where should I get my costume and makeup?" she asked.

The photographer looked confused. "I'm very busy," he said. "Why don't you just wait over there, Angela."

"It's *Angelica*," she said, rolling her eyes.

Chapter 6

Meanwhile, the babies had arrived at the greenroom door.

"Okay, guys," whispered Tommy. "I'm gonna open this door, and we're gonna get my brother before he gets sent to space! Ready?"

"Ready!" his friends replied.

Tommy pushed open the door very slowly. They all peeked in. Grandpa Lou was asleep in a puffy green chair.

The babies tiptoed inside.

"Oh, no!" said Chuckie.

Dil Pickles was nowhere to be found!

"Maybe it's too late," Lil said sadly.

"Maybe *we* were too late," said Phil.

"Maybe he's already in outside space, Tommy," said Chuckie.

Tommy wasn't ready to give up yet. "We gotta find Dil no matter what!" he shouted. "Follow me."

The babies turned around to leave . . . and bumped into four scaly green legs! They belonged to the aliens they'd seen leaving the greenroom! "Aaaaaah!" the babies screamed in unison.

"What are you kids doing here?" asked one of the aliens. "It's probably not a good idea for you to be walking around by yourselves here."

The aliens escorted the babies to a playpen in another part of the studio.

"You'll be much happier here," said one alien. With that, the two aliens walked away.

The babies looked around.

"Where are we?" said Chuckie.

"I think we've been kidnapped by aliums!" answered Tommy.

"Maybe we're in outside space," said Phil.

Suddenly the playpen started to rock. The photo studio disappeared. All around them was dark sky. There were stars everywhere.

"Captain Tommy reporting for duty!" Tommy shouted as he grabbed the steering wheel of the rocket ship. "Captain Chuckie, are you with me?"

"Roger, Captain Tommy," Chuckie said, peering at his friend through a space helmet with built-in glasses.

"We're here too," cried Phil and Lil.

They wore space suits over their diapers.

"We're on a special mission to save Dil," Tommy told his crew. "We gots to find him and get back to Earth in time for cartoons on TB!"

The babies' rocket ship sailed through the sky at high speeds. When they passed the man in the moon, Chuckie waved!

"He looks kinda like your grandpa Lou," Chuckie told Tommy.

"Maybe the moon is made of cheese!" said Phil. "Then we could eat it!"

"I'd rather have belly button lint," said Lil.

"No time for snacks, guys," said Captain Tommy. "We need to fly to find my brother. Everyone hang on!"

Tommy loved being the captain of the spaceship. He made a sharp turn. The babies bounced up, down, and around as they flew through space. "Captain Chuckie," said Tommy. "How long until we get back to Earth?"

"Looks like a billion more seconds! Just in time for Reptar on TB!" said Chuckie.

Just then another spaceship pulled up next to them.

"Uh-oh," said Tommy. "Looks like we gots another spaceship that wants to race with us!"

So the babies kicked the spaceship into high gear and were off on a race. They dipped to the left, and spun to the right, but the other ship was right on their tail!

"Gosh," said Chuckie. "Where do you think that driver's from?"

Lil looked out the window at the red, white, and blue flag painted on the side of the other ship. "He must be from

outside space. He gots stars painted on his spaceship," she said.

That spaceship could go fast! But with special maneuvering, the babies won their race. They were the number one riders in space!

All they had to do now was find Dil and get back to Earth. But something floating ahead in the distance was getting in their way.

Chapter 7

"Hey, you guys," said Captain Tommy. "Hang on to your diapies! We gots a problem up ahead!"

"What kinda problem, Tommy?" asked Chuckie.

Just then a giant meatball splattered against the windshield of their rocket ship. Another one followed. The ship rocked as meatballs hit it from all sides.

"I think it's a meat-eater shower!

Everybody take cover!" Tommy said as he grabbed the steering wheel.

"I wish I had some pasghetti," said Lil.

"Or worms," added Phil.

Captain Tommy navigated the spaceship through the sky like a pro. Soon the ship stopped rocking.

"Is everything okay?" asked Chuckie.

"Not yet," answered Tommy. "Looks like there are some aliums up ahead."

Chuckie didn't like the sound of that.

Ahead in the distance two aliens were flying through space in their own rocket ship. Their ship was big and green and looked like a huge egg. There were windows all around the egg, so the babies could see the aliens inside. They had pointy ears and big eyes, just like the aliens in the photo studio.

"Do they look like mean aliums?" asked Chuckie, who had covered his eyes.

"Can't tell from here, Captain Chuckie," shouted Tommy. "But we'll get by them. We gots a baby brother to save."

The babies sailed through the star-filled sky, heading straight toward the aliens. Tommy realized that one of the stars might be his own brother, Dil! Maybe I can ask the aliums for directions, thought Tommy.

When they got closer to the alien ship, Chuckie hid behind Phil and Lil.

The aliens stuck their heads out of their spaceship windows. "Can we help you?" they asked together.

"We're looking for a star named Dil. He's my little brother. Have you seen him?" asked Tommy.

"Just one second," the aliens said together. Then they stuck their long necks back inside their spaceship for a discussion.

"Whaddya think they're talking about?" asked Phil.

"Hopefully not babynapping us," said Chuckie.

The aliens reappeared. "We think he's in Kiddie Space. We happen to know an excellent shortcut," said the aliens. "Why don't you follow us?"

"We'll be right behind you!" said Captain Tommy.

And off they went.

They spiraled through the sky at record speeds! They swooshed past planets and zigzagged through clusters of stars.

"Those aliums sure like to drive fast!" said Chuckie.

All the babies hung on as Tommy flew them around the universe. It was hard to keep up with the aliens, but Tommy stayed right behind them. He knew that soon he'd find his little brother and bring him back to Earth.

All of a sudden a field of stars was in sight! The aliens stuck their heads out the window and pointed below, showing them where to land.

"We'll take it from here!" shouted Tommy.

And with that, the aliens took off back into the night.

The babies' spaceship landed with a thud.

"I think we're here," said Tommy.

The babies all jumped out of the spaceship. But none of them knew where they were!

Chapter 8

"Are we still in outside space?" asked Lil.

Tommy had no idea where they were. It was dark, and he didn't see anything he had seen before.

"I'm hungry!" wailed Lil.

"No, *I'm* hungry, Lillian!" shouted Philip.

"Waaaaaaaah," they both cried.

"I don't like it here, Tommy," said Chuckie. "I want to go home."

Tommy didn't know what to do. He

didn't like it much there, either. But he knew he had to be brave. "Listen, guys," he said. "This is our last chance to save Dil. We have to keep going!"

"But we don't even know *where* we're going, Tommy!" said Chuckie. "We don't even know where we are."

"We know where we are," said Phil. "We're lost."

"And hungry," added Lil.

Tommy thought for a moment. "Maybe the aliums gave us the wrong directions," he said. "Maybe we're on the Moon!"

"Well, how do we get back?" asked Lil.

Tommy thought of how he had seen the Moon high in the sky at night.

"We just gotta head downstairs to find Earth," he said.

"That's easy," said Phil. "Look over there!" Phil was pointing to a small staircase.

"All right, guys," said Tommy. "All we

gotta do is walk from the Moon to the Earth. We can do it!"

The babies started crawling backward down the stairs from the Moon back to Earth. Soon the stars began to fade from the sky. In no time, the sky was gone. The babies looked around. They were back in the photo studio.

"Hooray! We're back on Earth!" Phil and Lil cheered.

"In time for TB!" added Chuckie.

But Tommy wasn't happy. "We didn't find Dil," he said sadly. "Now my brother's stuck in space forever and ever, just like Angelica said."

But no sooner had Tommy spoken than he spotted Angelica standing by the photographer in the distance. And right next to them, who was curled up in a rocket shaped like a pickle? It was Dil!

"Look!" said Tommy. "It's Dil! He hasn't been shot into space yet after all!"

The babies had flown through space and walked on the Moon! And now they still had time to save Dil!

"You sprouts having fun?" Grandpa Lou asked as he picked Tommy up out of the playpen and set him on the floor.

Chapter 9

Angelica was not having much fun. Everyone was cooing and paying attention to dumb Dil. Hadn't the director said Angelica was something else? Didn't he know he was making a mistake?

"Let's get this moving, people," shouted the photographer. "Let's get the aliens in place. And get a jar of pickles to put by the rocket ship."

People were running all over the place.

"Where are the pickles?" shouted the photographer. "I need someone to get the pickles!"

"Angelica Pickles, at your service!" she said sweetly to the photographer.

And then she was off to find a jar of pickles. She knew that this might be her last chance to be their star. But her stomach was rumbling. She hadn't had a snack.

The pickles sure look good, she thought. Maybe if I just have one little pickle. . . .

Angelica popped open the jar and crunched on a pickle. It tasted good! If she just had one more, nobody would notice.

Angelica happily munched . . . until she ate the whole jar!

The babies crawled quickly toward the pickle-shaped rocket ship.

"There he is, guys," yelled Tommy. "There's my baby brother!"

The babies all rushed to Dil's side. They had come a long way to save Dil, and they weren't leaving no matter what!

"Hey, Tommy, look!" said Chuckie. "How did the aliums get here?"

The two aliens with the pointy ears and big eyes were standing behind Dil.

"Let's get ready to shoot!" shouted the photographer.

Dil gurgled.

"Oh, no!" Tommy cried.

The photographer was standing behind his camera. Dil was about to be shot into outer space! There was little time left!

"Let's get him outta here!" shouted Tommy.

And with that, the babies climbed up

the pickle rocket ship to Dil's rescue.

"Wait!" shouted the photographer. Everyone in the studio froze. It was so quiet, you could hear a pin drop. "Where did those four babies come from?" he asked.

Everyone stared at the babies.

"They are perfect! I want all of them. SHOOT!" he screamed.

Before the babies could even blink, the camera clicked.

There was a thunderous display of lights! The babies couldn't see a thing.

Then there was silence.

"What happened, Tommy?" asked Chuckie. "Are we in outside space again?"

"You kids are perfect!" shouted the photographer. "You four are going to be on every jar of Rocket Pickles and every poster in town! You babies are stars!"

"Let's get you babies home," Grandpa Lou said. "Your moms and dads are going to be so proud!"

"Did ya hear that, Chuckie?" said Tommy. "We're gonna be stars, and we don't even have to live in outside space! Angelica was wrong! This is the bestest day!"

For the babies it was a spectacular day filled with stars and rocket ships and pickles. But not for Angelica. She was stuck in the greenroom with an empty jar of pickles and a tummy ache. And the dumb babies were going to be stars.

Angelica let out a deep sigh. Who wanted to be on a dumb jar of pickles, anyway?

YOU CAN ENTER FOR A CHANCE TO WIN A TRIP FOR FOUR TO NICKELODEON STUDIOS® FLORIDA!

1 GRAND PRIZE:
A 3-day/2-night trip for four to Nickelodeon Studios in Orlando, Florida

3 FIRST PRIZES:
A Sony Playstation® system and a *Rugrats™ in Paris* Playstation game from THQ®

25 SECOND PRIZES:
A *The Wild Thornberrys* CD-ROM from Mattel Interactive

100 THIRD PRIZES:
A set of four books from Simon & Schuster Children's Publishing, including a *The Wild Thornberrys* title, a *Rugrats* title, a *SpongeBob SquarePants* title, and a *Hey Arnold!* title

Complete entry form and send to:
Simon & Schuster Children's Publishing Division
Marketing Department/ "Nickelodeon Studios Florida Sweepstakes"
1230 Avenue of the Americas, 4th Floor, NY, NY 10020

Name_____ Birthdate___/___/_____

Address_____

City_____ State_____ Zip_____

Phone (____) _____

Parent/Guardian Signature _____

Simon & Schuster Children's Publishing Division/ "Nickelodeon Studios Florida Sweepstakes" Sponsor's Official Rules:

NO PURCHASE NECESSARY.

Enter by mailing this completed Official Entry Form (no copies allowed) or by mailing a 3 1/2" x 5" card with your complete name and address, parent and/or legal guardian's name, daytime telephone number, and birthdate to the Simon & Schuster Children's Publishing Division/ "Nickelodeon Studios Florida Sweepstakes," 1230 Avenue of the Americas, 4th Floor, NY, NY 10020. Entry forms are available in the back of *The Rugrats Files #3: The Quest for the Holey Pail* (12/2000), *Rugrats Chapter Book #10: Dil in a Pickle* (11/2000), *The Wild Thornberrys Chapter Book #2: Two Promises Too Many!* (9/2000), *The Wild Thornberrys Chapter Book #3: A Time to Share* (9/2000), *SpongeBob SquarePants Trivia Book* (9/2000), *SpongeBob SquarePants Joke Book* (9/2000), *Hey Arnold! Chapter Book #1: Arnold for President* (9/2000), and *Hey Arnold! Chapter Book #2: Return of the Sewer King* (9/2000), and on the web site SimonSaysKids.com. Sweepstakes begins 8/1/2000 and ends 2/28/2001. Entries must be postmarked by 2/28/01 and received by 3/15/01. Not responsible for lost, late, damaged, postage-due, stolen, illegible, mutilated, incomplete, or misdirected or not delivered entries or mail, or for typographical errors in the entry form or rules. Entries are void if they are in whole or in part illegible, incomplete, or damaged. Enter as often as you wish, but each entry must be mailed separately. Entries will not be returned. Winners will be selected at random from all eligible entries received in a drawing to be held on or about 3/30/01. Grand prize winner must be available to travel during the months of June and July 2001. If Grand Prize winner is unable to travel on the specified dates, prize will be forfeited and awarded to an alternate. Winners will be notified by mail within 30 days of selection. The grand prize winner will be notified by phone as well. Odds of winning depend on the number of eligible entries received.

Prizes: One Grand Prize: A 3-day/2-night trip for four to Nickelodeon Studios in Orlando, FL, including a VIP tour, admission for four to Universal Studios Florida, round-trip coach airfare from a major U.S. airport nearest the winner's residence, and standard hotel accommodations (2 rooms, double occupancy) of sponsor's choice. (Total approx. retail value: $2,700.00). Winner must be accompanied by a parent or legal guardian. Prize does not include transfers, gratuities, or any other expenses not specified or listed herein. 3 First Prizes: A Sony Playstation system and a *Rugrats* Playstation game from THQ. (Total approx. retail value: $150.00 each). 25 Second Prizes: A *The Wild Thornberrys* CD-ROM from Mattel Interactive. (Approx. retail value: $29.99 each). 100 Third Prizes: A set of four books from Simon & Schuster Children's Publishing, including a *The Wild Thornberrys* title, a *Rugrats* title, a *SpongeBob SquarePants* title, and a *Hey Arnold!* title. (Total approx. retail value: $12.00 per set).

The sweepstakes is open to legal residents of the continental U.S. (excluding Puerto Rico) and Canada (excluding Quebec) ages 5-13 as of 2/28/01. Proof of age is required to claim prize. Prizes will be awarded to winner's parent or legal guardian. Void wherever prohibited or restricted by law. All provincial, federal, state, and local laws apply. Simon & Schuster Inc. and MTV Networks and their respective officers, directors, shareholders, employees, suppliers, parent companies, subsidiaries, affiliates, agencies, sponsors, participating retailers, and persons connected with the use, marketing, or conducting of this sweepstakes are not eligible. Family members living in the same household as any of the individuals referred to in the preceding sentence are not eligible.

One prize per person or household. Prizes are not transferable, have no cash equivalent, and may not be substituted except by sponsors, in the event of prize unavailability, in which case a prize of equal or greater value will be awarded. All prizes will be awarded.

If a winner is a Canadian resident, then he/she must correctly answer a skill-based question administered by mail.

All expenses on receipt and use of prize including provincial, federal, state, and local taxes are the sole responsibility of the winner's parent or legal guardian. Winners' parents or legal guardians may be required to execute and return an Affidavit of Eligibility and Publicity Release and all other legal documents which the sweepstakes sponsors may require (including a W-9 tax form) within 15 days of attempted notification or an alternate winner will be selected. The grand prize winner, parent or legal guardian, and travel companions will be required to execute a liability release form prior to ticketing.

Winners' parents or legal guardians on behalf of the winners agree to allow use of winners' names, photographs, likenesses, and entries for any advertising, promotion, and publicity purposes without further compensation to or permission from the entrants, except where prohibited by law.

Winners and winners' parents or legal guardians agree that Simon & Schuster, Inc., Nickelodeon Studios, THQ, and MTV Networks and their respective officers, directors, shareholders, employees, suppliers, parent companies, subsidiaries, affiliates, agencies, sponsors, participating retailers, and persons connected with the use, marketing, or conducting of this sweepstakes shall have no responsibility or liability for injuries, losses, or damages of any kind in connection with the collection, acceptance, or use of the prizes awarded herein, or from participation in this promotion.

By participating in this sweepstakes, entrants agree to be bound by these rules and the decisions of the judges and sweepstakes sponsors, which are final in all matters relating to the sweepstakes. Failure to comply with the Official Rules may result in a disqualification of your entry and prohibition of any further participation in this sweepstakes.

The first names of the winners will be posted at SimonSaysKids.com or the first names of the winners may be obtained by sending a stamped, self-addressed envelope after 3/30/01 to Prize Winners, Simon & Schuster Children's Publishing Division "Nickelodeon Studios Sweepstakes," 1230 Avenue of the Americas, 4th Floor, NY, NY 10020.

Sponsor of sweepstakes is Simon & Schuster Inc.